THE EYE

Cyrus Spielberg

Cyrus Spielberg

Copyright © Statement

No part of this book may be reproduced or transmitted in any form or by any means, electronic or mechanical, including recording, photocopying, or by any information storage and retrieval system, without the written permission of the publisher.

The Eye

Cyrus Spielberg

Table of Contents

CHAPTER ONE – BOMBAY 1765 5

CHAPTER TWO – BOMBAY - LONDON - AFRICA- 1767 22

CHAPTER THREE – AFRICA, VIRGINIA- 1768..39

CHAPTER FOUR - AFRICA - 1780...53

CHAPTER FIVE - LONDON - 1781 57

CHAPTER SIX – VIRGINIA, AMERICA - 1790 61

CHAPTER SEVEN- LONDON, VIRGINIA, JERUSALEM, BOMBAY AND TIBET - 1792 71

ACKNOWLEDGEMENTS 89

Chapter One – Bombay 1765

The clock of St Thomas Cathedral chimed midnight on All Hallows Eve breaking the silence within the temple which was situated off a secluded alleyway not far from Bombay's port. By day the port was a hive of activity, by night it was a ghost town.

Illuminated by the full moon a jagged-edged silver blade dripped blood from its tip, the warm ruby red liquid splashing in tiny droplets at the feet of he who had brandished the knife so mercilessly.

The ritual sacrifice of the now mutilated goat's body had been performed by Major Henry Clive at the feet of a statue of the Goddess Jinn. An all-seeing eye necklace hung from the major's neck, swinging in full view of his fellow cult members, whose own eyes were transfixed on the ritual slaughter. Major Henry's eyes were vacant, as though in a trance, his whole being possessed as he channelled the desires of their goddess. Fixated on his every move, the congregation watched him, utterly spellbound, embracing and sensing his every move, absorbing all that this sacred ceremonial meant to them.

Two years hence the same cursed blade would claim the life of Elizabeth Goldsmith in the most horrific of circumstances and for no other reason than desire. The followers of the Goddess Jinn made no exception when it came to sacrifice, not even for those whose hearts were pure.

***

Jacob Goldsmith was a tall handsome man, of muscular build, with light brown hair. An English officer of the East India Company, Jacob had been stationed in India under the leadership of Major Henry Clive. He had travelled east with his wife Elizabeth and their five-year-old daughter Sarah to settle in Bombay earlier that year.

Jacob Goldsmith and Elizabeth Blum were both descendants of Jewish merchants who had been granted permission to come to the UK a century before, to help rebuild the economy following the devastation of the Civil War. Within a close knit and affluent Jewish community, Jacob and Elizabeth had grown up together and always attended the same events and gatherings. The Goldsmith boys, Jacob and his brother Michael, had for all intents and purposes adopted Elizabeth as their younger sister. Living so close to one another they had shared many adventures together in the City of London, as well as on excursions to the surrounding countryside.

As the years went by, and the boy became a man, Jacob realised that his feelings for Elizabeth were more than just platonic. Every day that he spent with Elizabeth, who daily seemed to grow ever more breathtakingly beautiful, Jacob fell deeper and deeper in love with her. One evening, as they said goodnight to one another, Jacob took Elizabeth's hand in his, looked in to her eyes, and finally confessed that his feelings for her were more than friendship, that he was completely in love with her and could not imagine spending a single day without her.

Whilst growing up Jacob and Elizabeth had been taught by their respective families the importance of charity and helping those less fortunate than themselves. It was something so deeply rooted inside of them that it became a natural instinct and something which they continued throughout their marriage, both in London and when they relocated to India.

***

Jacob and Elizabeth took to life in Bombay with ease, mingling with the English aristocracy who also found themselves in the employ of the East India Company and poste overseas. Everywhere Elizabeth went, her beauty commanded the attention of all who looked upon her. She was at ease with everyone she met, regardless of their status, their ego or their ignorance. Elizabeth looked only for ways she could benefit others, almost communicating with the souls of the people she encountered. There was, however, one exception to this. Major Henry Clive.

Working alongside Jacob, Major Henry was very much a part of his and Elizabeth's lives and although Elizabeth found Henry to behave in a manner which was to be expected of him, always looking the part and fulfilling his role with gusto, there was something about him that made her wary. His smooth talking, immaculate uniform and authoritative presence was admired and accepted by all, but not by Elizabeth. If she had been asked to identify what it was that made her feel this way she could not have explained it, but she felt uneasy in his presence and that there was something sinister he was hiding. Where Elizabeth saw only light and goodness in others, she sensed a darkness in Henry which unnerved her. Whenever they did meet she had a feeling which she could only have described as a butterfly trapped in her stomach and she would always excuse herself from his presence as soon as was polite.

***

The large house, in the heart of Bombay, which Elizabeth and Jacob called home, was full of people. Preparations for that evening's event had been going on for several weeks but Elizabeth was confident that all would go to plan when Bombay's finest gathered later that day for her fundraising gala.

Jacob had ventured out that morning, promising to return as soon as he could to assist his wife with the final preparations, but as Elizabeth kissed her husband goodbye she had been struck by a sense of foreboding and she was struggling to shake off her discomfort.

Jacob had commissioned a unique piece of jewellery for Elizabeth, which he was planning to present to her that night. He had worked with Bombay's finest jeweller to design a gold locket with a peacock etched into the precious metal and a flawless ruby for the bird's eye. The piece was not quite ready when Jacob called on the jeweller that morning, so tingling with excitement, he left the jeweller to finish the piece and walked home along the main street. Grinning to himself as he strode confidently down the road, Jacob was aware of the differing sounds all around him, including his own his boot buckles which rattled with his every step. His attention was diverted suddenly to a group of noisy children, close to a textile warehouse, who had formed a circle around a small boy and were preventing his escape.

"Stop it! Stop it!" The youth shouted at the human shield. Jacob could see that the boy had something in his hand which the other children seemed intent on taking.

"No! No! Stop it!" The boy shouted again, then one of the children jumped forward trying to grab the item, creating a tiny gap in the human circle. The boy seized the opportunity, put his head down and charged towards the space. Once outside the group he looked up and ran directly towards Jacob. The circle of children dispersed, fleeing in all directions as the escapee, panting, revealed the item that had caused such a commotion. As his eyes focused, Jacob immediately recognised the object; it was his gold pocket watch, with a portrait of Elizabeth inside.

"You dropped this sir," explained the boy, extending his hand to return the item.

"Thank you," Jacob responded, looking at the small boy's striking emerald green eyes and his innocent grubby face. Jacob was well aware that had it not been for this boy, his pocket watch would have been lost to him forever, traded by the street children for food. This little urchin was different it seemed.

"What is your name child?" asked Jacob, crouching down so that he might speak eye to eye with the boy.

"My name is Raja sir," answered the boy, "I saw you drop your pocket watch sir and I picked it up, so I could return it to you sir, but the others sir, the others came out of nowhere sir, and tried to stop me from giving it back to you sir."

Raja had clearly suffered at the hands of these others and Jacob's heart went out to this child who wore rags for clothes and whose feet were bare and filthy.

"You are a very brave and honest boy to do such a thing Raja." Jacob kneeled as he spoke so as to be eye-to-eye with the boy.

"Thank you, sir," said Raja "but I was just doing what my mother taught me to do, she always taught me to do the right thing and the right thing was to give you back your pocket watch sir." Jacob had caught the flicker of pain in the boys eyes at the mention of his mother.

"Where is your mother Raja? I would like to thank her too for raising such a fine young man." Jacob eyed the boys cuts and grazes and hoped he had been wrong in thinking originally that the boy was an orphan.

Raja looked at his feet as he hung his head.

"My mother died sir. She was all the family I had and now I have no one," replied Raja quite matter-of-factly.

"Then you must come home with me," said Jacob without hesitation.

"Why sir?" exclaimed Raja, hesitant as to what Jacob had in mind.

"Well I am certain that my wife would like to also thank you for returning this to me, she gave it to me on our wedding day, so it is very precious. After that I think you could perhaps benefit from a bath and maybe a change of clothes, also a decent meal. How is that for starters?"

Raja beamed from ear to ear.
"Yes sir!" he smiled, looking fit to burst with pride and anticipation.

As they walked back to the house they chatted, their conversation flowing as though they had known each other all their lives. Several sets of brown eyes belonging to the recently dispersed street children watched with curiosity as Raja and Jacob continued along the street to Jacob's house. The maid that opened the door took Raja to the kitchen to get him cleaned up a bit and give him some food, while Jacob went to find Elizabeth.

"Hello darling," Jacob smiled as Elizabeth turned towards him, away from the table plan she was working on.

"I've missed you," Elizabeth replied, walking over to her husband and kissing him gently on his cheek.

They sat next to each other on a window seat as Jacob relayed the story of his pocket watch and his encounter with Raja.

"I must go and meet this little angel and thank him myself. Where can we find him?" Elizabeth enquired.

Jacob held his wife's hand.

"Actually, I brought him home with me, I knew you would want to meet him and I think I would like for him to stay with us, if you wouldn't mind?"

Elizabeth could see in her husband's eyes that this was something which was very important to him.

"If it is what you want to do, you know you have my full support in all things." She could not refuse him such a humanitarian request.

Smiling Jacob squeezed her hand, then like a small child himself Jacob ran to find Raja and tell him the good news.

***

Major Henry Clive was one of the first to arrive for the fundraising event that evening, turning up ahead of all the other guests with his silent auction donation, a beautiful watercolour painting, which was placed by a member of staff on a table in the main hall. Henry took a drink from one of the waiters and went over to peruse the table plan. Henry smiled to himself when he saw that he would be sharing the largest of the round tables with several other guests which included the hosts Jacob and Elizabeth.

Other guests began to arrive, all of Bombay's elite had been invited, and it was not long before the room was alive with the sound of voices and laughter. Jacob returned home, having run an errand, with the fundraising event in full swing. Immediately catching Elizabeth's eye for a moment, he heard nothing except the pounding of his own heart expressing his love for her.

"Over here!" Someone shouted from across the room, taking Jacob's focus away from his beautiful wife who looked radiant in a sapphire blue taffeta gown.

Waving enthusiastically with one hand, raising a glass of wine in the other, a guest showed Jacob to his table. The evening surpassed all expectations as the generous bidding continued long into the night. Midnight came and went as the guests gravitated to the dance area. Exhausted from her long day and happy with the evening's success, Elizabeth slipped away from the mansion into the garden for a few moments to herself. Finding a garden bench Elizabeth sat down, kicked off her shoes and rested her eyes for a moment, recalling moments from the evening and smiling to herself at a job well done. When she opened her eyes, she was surprised to find Pari sat next to her on the bench, for she had not heard her approach. Unbeknownst to Elizabeth, Pari was an evil sorceress and the wife of one of the cults most senior members.

"You must be delighted with this evening's event Elizabeth, what a wonderful success," Pari said, looking deep into Elizabeth's eyes as she spoke.

"I couldn't be happier!" Elizabeth replied, reclining again and closing her eyes.

"You must be exhausted though; these things take such a lot of preparation."

"I must confess to feeling a little tired," admitted Elizabeth.

Silently Pari stood and moved behind Elizabeth and

started to gently massage her neck and shoulders. Elizabeth instantly relaxed and drifted into a dreamlike state, faintly aware of a soft melodic sound she had never heard before. Pari's voice was indeed barely audible. Elizabeth could not have known that Pari was, in fact, chanting and casting a spell on her.

Excusing herself by telling Elizabeth that her husband was calling for her, although Elizabeth had heard nothing, Pari went over to a nearby tree on which hung a highly decorated birdcage containing a blackbird. Pari retrieved from her pocket a tiny scroll of paper on which was written a prayer, then using a strand of Elizabeth's hair, which had been easily removed, Pari wrapped the scroll around the blackbird's leg. Taking the bird in her hands she whispered a final enchantment as she released it and it flew away deep into the garden, perfectly camouflaged by the darkness.

The spell had been cast upon Elizabeth at the request of Major Henry Clive, and if successful would mean that she would now desire him. It was to Major Henry that Pari went directly from the garden.

"It is done, Elizabeth will be yours now, she will desire you as you instructed for as long as the blackbird lives."

***

Over the next few weeks, the fundraising evening was

the talk of the town. Jacob and Elizabeth were warmly welcomed and congratulated everywhere they went for the success of their event. But Jacob began to see a change in Elizabeth and observed her giving more and more attention to Henry, where previously she had not. Jacob had these thoughts whirring around his head one morning as he walked briskly along the road, trying to keep pace with Raja. They shared a relaxed conversation as he escorted Raja to school for the very first time. Feeling like a king Raja held Jacob's hand, proud of his smart new clothes and shoes. Nearing the school building, Raja's grip intensified, Jacob assumed the boy was nervous despite his words to the contrary. On arrival, a teacher was there waiting to welcome Raja to the school.

"Good Morning Raja," the teacher smiled, "my name is Mr Johnson, please put your bag here," he continued, pointing at an empty metal peg.

"Good Morning Mr Johnson," Raja responded in a very quiet voice, placing his bag on the peg as instructed. While Jacob chatted to Mr Johnson in the hallway Raja drifted a short distance away looking at the displays on the walls. Any reservations that Jacob or Raja may have had however, evaporated when Jacob saw the boy engaging with a group of children his own age. Jacob's heart warmed at the welcome received by Raja and he went home smiling to himself.

***

Sarah and Raja, being similar in age, become inseparable; they even created their own secret language. They shared a love of music and practised daily. Sarah was an accomplished pianist for her age and had introduced Raja to the violin. With no formal lessons and unable to read music, Raja was a natural, teaching himself to play by ear, feeling the sounds using his senses.

The mansion was a fantastic playground for the children offering an abundance of hiding places for one of their favourite games. When permitted by Sarah and Raja, Jacob would join in with their games of hide and seek. Entering the children's innocent world of wonder kept a healthy life balance for him. Whenever he played with Sarah and Raja it was like déjà vu, taking him right back to the time when he and Elizabeth, together with his brother Michael, had played games together as children.

***

Jacob was informed by his superior, Major Henry Clive, that he was required to go to another city to work for a while and it was with much reluctance that he was forced to follow orders and leave his wife and the children behind. The major's motives were purely to remove Jacob for a while for the spell on Elizabeth to work its dark magic unhindered by the presence of one who loved her.

Using Jacob's absence to his advantage, the major visited Elizabeth at every opportunity, under the pretext that it was his duty to make sure she was faring well while her husband was away. All the while, the darkness within Henry guided his every move, until one night it manifested itself.

Elizabeth was returning home from having spent the afternoon at a local orphanage at which she volunteered. It was later than usual for her to be out and dusk was already falling on the city as she walked the short distance home. Elizabeth had not gone very far when she became aware of footsteps behind her. Quickening her pace, the footsteps followed suit, but when she turned to see who was there, no one was in sight. Feeling uneasy Elizabeth continued on her way, maintaining a brisk pace and as she turned the corner always occupied by an armless beggar, she ran headlong in to Major Henry, almost stumbling into his arms.

"Oh, thank goodness it's you, Henry!" Elizabeth smiled in relief, her body shaking visibly as she took a respectful step back from Henry.

Henry took her trembling hand.

"What's wrong? Are you on your way home?" he enquired.

Looking behind her once again, Elizabeth saw no one and returned her gaze to Henry.
"You are shaking like a leaf my dear."

"Oh Major, I thought I heard someone following me, it has unnerved me somewhat," she replied.

"You need a brandy," Henry insisted and still holding onto her immaculately manicured hand, he led her to his house.

Elizabeth had never been alone with Henry before, nor had she been to his house.

Henry showed her in to an austere but comfortable drawing room and poured two glasses of brandy, passing one to Elizabeth. Still trembling she lifted the glass to her lips and felt the warmth of the alcohol spread around her body as she drank.

"Thank you," she smiled, feeling a little calmer, completely unaware of the vulnerable position into which she had been unwittingly ensnared.

Elizabeth found the intimacy of the situation unnerving but for some reason she was unable to excuse herself and make her way home. The next she knew, Henry was behind her, kissing her neck. Elizabeth froze, alarmed and yet somehow accepting of the situation despite herself. Elizabeth allowed Henry to unbutton her dress, and still she did not protest, she did not move. It was as though she was an observer, watching the events unfolding from above, as though it was happening to someone else. The major took Elizabeth for his own that night, while powerless to stop him she allowed herself to be taken and afterwards, as though it had been an ordinary evening, he walked her home. They only spoke to say good night to one another, and then Henry disappeared into the darkness.

The events of that night were never spoken of again.

***

Following a dry season, south westerly winds brought rain to Bombay, bringing change, mirroring the turmoil Elizabeth felt internally. She was days away from giving birth to her second child. Elizabeth painted a smile on her face every day and celebrated her joy with Jacob, but as the rain battered the delicate leaves of the plants in their garden Elizabeth's heart ached. Her secret was so powerful it invaded every cell of her body. It was only the spell that kept her from speaking out and her shame at what she had allowed to happen.

When the baby was born, the midwife rejoiced,

"It's a boy!" she cried, swaddling the child and handing over the noisy bundle to his mother.

Elizabeth looked into the eyes of her beautiful new creation. The face staring back at her was unmistakably Henry's. The baby had his thick black hair, it was quite obvious to Elizabeth that the father of her child was not her husband.

As the rain increased, the visitors to the house reduced. Henry had visited more than once and seen the baby, who Elizabeth and Jacob had named David, on several occasions. Each time he had given Elizabeth a knowing look. Their secret was poison to Elizabeth, infiltrating every part of her body. When she had the opportunity to be alone with Henry she tried to express her pain, but he always refused to listen, and she was forced to carry the burden of her guilt alone.

Chapter Two – Bombay - London – Africa - 1767

Six months later Jacob, Elizabeth, Sarah and new-born David were summoned back to the UK, along with other personnel, including Major Henry Clive. Their belongings were packed up and they prepared for months at sea as they began the long journey home. Jacob had arranged for Raja to stay in Bombay with a local family to continue his schooling, funded by him. It was with much sadness that Elizabeth and Jacob had to say goodbye to the child who had become like one of their own.

Jacob could not help but notice the change in Elizabeth, although he put it down to pressures of motherhood and the exhaustion that went with it. He hoped that once they were settled back in London, perhaps things would improve.

Not long after their return to the UK, Elizabeth organised a ball to which she invited senior personnel who had returned from India with them. Thousands of miles away in India, on the very same day, the blackbird, with the spell still wrapped around its leg, was attacked by a local cat and perished on the doorstep of the evil sorceress Pari's home. The spell was now broken.

Henry had long been concerned that Elizabeth would at some point reveal what had happened between them that night in Bombay when David was conceived. He had enlisted the help of a fellow cult member, Alistair Stafford, equally as dark as he, to deal with the problem and together they had devised an evil plan to prevent the truth of David's parentage ever being revealed. At the ball Henry immediately noticed the change in Elizabeth and knew that he had been right to make prior arrangements to prevent her revealing his dark secrets.

Alistair too worked for the East India Company in London. Whilst so many of his colleagues had been temporarily transferred to India, he had needed to remain in the UK to take care of his family's estate, one which he was in line to inherit as the only Stafford son. Alistair had an illegitimate son named Stan, the result of regular visits to Madame Scarlet, the owner of a public house and brothel in London's Covent Garden.

Elizabeth and Jacobs's event that evening was a huge success as expected, providing the first opportunity for those recently returned from India to assemble all in one place and relive happy memories of their time in the East.

As the dining ended, the dancing began, and Alistair slipped away alone from the main event to the drawing room, where drinks were being served. He asked the barman for a round of port for his companions and was presented with a tray holding several crystal glasses each containing the fortified wine. When no one was looking he carefully added three drops of a powerful sedative to the glass closest to his left hand and returned to the room full of dancing guests. He went straight over to his target and rested the tray on the table where Jacob was seated, in deep conversation with another officer.

"Would you gentlemen join me in a glass of port?" Alistair asked, interrupting their flow. Without waiting for a response Alistair carefully placed the tainted glass of port in front of Jacob and distributed the rest to the other guests. The conversation continued, and as Jacob tipped his head back to allow the last of the port to slip down his throat, Alistair noticed Jacob's eyes starting to roll back. Realising the sedative was taking effect instantly, Alistair put Jacob's arm around his neck and raised him from his chair.

"Come on Jacob, let's get you to bed, looks like you've had too much to drink tonight," Alistair announced to the rest of the table, as he supported a very unsteady Jacob against his body. Jacob was confused and tried to ask questions as Alistair took him upstairs to his bedroom, but the words were slurred and the drug inside of him forced his heavy eyelids to close. Alistair quickly undressed Jacob, leaving him unconscious in his own bed.

Meanwhile, with Jacob out of the way, Henry pulled Elizabeth on to the dance floor before she had a chance to refuse and not wanting to make a scene in front of her guests, she was reluctantly led around the floor, with a smile on her face which masked her true feelings. When the dance ended Elizabeth tried to pull away, but Henry kept hold of her arm and escorted her from the room towards the garden, threatening her that if she did not leave quietly with him then harm would come to Jacob and their daughter Sarah.

Outside they were met by Alistair. The night was especially dark as thick cloud and fog blanketed the city, hiding the moon and stars, and the ritual sacrifice that was about to take place. Despite the darkness, Alistair and Henry, with Elizabeth imprisoned between them, easily found their way to the temple, even with no light to guide them.

Henry had decided that the only way to prevent Elizabeth from speaking out about their occult activities and the child conceived as a result, was by silencing her forever. Under the watchful eyes of the assembled cult members, Elizabeth struggled as she was gagged, bound and laid at the feet of the statue of Goddess Jinn.

Henry instructed Alistair to perform the sacrifice of Elizabeth and entering a trance-like state, Alistair became instantly possessed, his eyes vacant. As the other cult members chanted and moved their bodies in ecstasy, using the ceremonial blade that Henry had brought back with him from Bombay, Alistair slit Elizabeth's throat, carved out her heart and consumed it. The group raised their arms in unison as they celebrated the sacrifice they were giving to their goddess, drinking the warm blood that poured from Elizabeth's open wounds.

Alistair wrapped Elizabeth's mutilated body in a rug and lifted her from the blood-soaked table. The darkness was to Alistair's advantage as he carried Elizabeth home, completely unnoticed. The party guests had long since ventured home and the staff had retired to their beds. It seemed no one had realised that both the host and hostess had vanished. Once in the house, Alistair climbed the stairs, as he had done earlier that evening with Jacob. Entering the master bedroom Alistair could see that Jacob was still out cold from the drug given to him earlier. Alistair laid Elizabeth's body on the bed next to Jacob's, unwrapped her from the blood-soaked rug and placed the bloodied knife next to her. He then smeared some of Elizabeth's blood onto Jacob's hands and clothes, completing the evil task he and Henry had devised to frame Jacob for her murder.

Sunshine welcomed in the next day, and as the maid opened the curtains of her master's bedroom, the rays of sunlight flooded in to reveal the horrific sight of Elizabeth's mutilated body on the bed and Jacob's blood-stained body still sleeping next to her. Frozen to the spot the maid screamed, waking Jacob instantly. Confused and bleary eyed, trying to remember how he had got into bed the previous night, it took Jacob a moment to realise that he was covered in blood and that next to him lay Elizabeth's lifeless body, slashed and torn, more blood than he had ever before seen soaked into the bed sheets.

The maid ran from the room screaming for someone to help while Jacob, not quite rid of the effects of the drugs and now in complete shock, could only hold his dead wife in his arms, heaving great sobs as he struggled to understand why and how this could have happened.

Time stood still for Jacob at that moment. He could not have said how long it was before a constable arrived having been fetched from the nearby magistrate's office by the maid.

Jacob was arrested, despite protesting his innocence, but the situation in which he and Elizabeth had been discovered was damning. His brother Michael appointed London's most reputable barrister to represent Jacob, but they soon learned that the judge who would be trying Jacob in court was a friend of Henry Clive and by now Jacob believed that Elizabeth's death had something to do with the major. The judge was in fact a member of Henry's cult and therefore benefitted from Jacob being made a scapegoat in the murder of his wife. It was obvious that Jacob would be found guilty and convicted of his wife's murder. They were running out of time and knew that the only way out would be for Jacob to escape and leave the country. They had a second cousin in Virginia, America, who they knew they could trust completely, his name was Adam Adelson. It was with him, they decided, that Jacob would be safe so Michael wrote him a letter and made plans for Jacob's escape from both prison and the country. Michael also took on guardianship of his niece and nephew Sarah and David, as the shockwaves from such a senseless death shattered the community in which they lived.

With the help of his brother, Jacob escaped his cell, and disguised as an Indian servant, made his way north to Liverpool and boarded a ship bound for America via Africa. On board he kept to himself, grieving the loss of his beautiful loving wife and trying to make sense of the madness he had left behind in London. The ship's cat, Jacob's only companion, would sit on his lap every evening, while Jacob petted him and told him of his woes. One night, Jacob was woken in his bunk by the shouts of the crew, panic evident in their voices. Up on deck, roaring thunder crashed overhead as forks of lightning illuminated the entire night sky.

A violent storm was turning the reasonably calm seas into towering walls of water which tossed the ship around as though it was made of paper, heaving the occupants from one side to the other, threatening to overthrow into the gloomy depths whosoever was brave or foolish enough to stand on deck. The ship surrendered itself to the deadly storm and started to break up with a cracking noise that sent even more fear into the hearts of the already terrified passengers and crew. Jacob fought his way to get on deck, losing his footing several times, flying objects hitting him from all directions. The sounds of shouting, gushing water, howling winds and the thunder assaulted his senses. Once on deck, Jacob gripped tightly to the handrail and as the ship filled rapidly with water, Jacob prayed to God.

The storm blew out as quickly as it had blown in but all that remained of the ship was either at the bottom of the ocean or floating on its now calm surface.

In open water, utterly exhausted, Jacob clung to the large piece of wood on which he was sprawled. Drifting in and out of consciousness, blood pouring from a cut on his head and bottom lip, he became aware of someone next to him, a sailor, but then suddenly everything turned black.

The following morning, as dawn broke, the light of the sun woke Jacob. Staring up at the clouds he managed to sit up and found himself on a piece of the wreckage. Beside him was a young man who he recognised as a member of the crew.

"It wasn't our day to die," said the man, smiling as he pointed to some land in the distance. All around them splintered wreckage, crates, luggage and various other items, which had once been the ships contents, decorated the surface of the sea.

"Where are we?" Jacob asked.

"Well by my reckoning, that's Africa over there. I'm Jack by the way."

"I'm Jacob," he replied, trying to return a smile without splitting his lip again. Jack explained how he was certain no one else had survived and fortunately for them the current was slowly drifting the wood towards the coast. Two days passed, the progress was slow, hunger, thirst and the heat of the sun caused the inevitable dehydration, which was now taking its toll. Both men were desperately weak and vulnerable, able only to lie on their temporary raft, occasionally whispering something to each other.

On land, local fishermen and pearl hunters were busy unloading their days catch. Their conversation focused mainly on the storm which had occurred two nights ago and the ship's debris which was washing up on shore. As the fishermen gazed out across the sea one of them pointed and shouted.

Jacob and Jack were faintly aware of voices shouting and prayed that the owners of the voices were mounting a rescue mission to come out to sea and save them.

The shipwrecked pair had indeed been spotted, their prayers answered.

The fishermen pushed two small boats into the water and headed towards the two men who lay listless and badly sunburnt on the broken piece of wood. It did not take long for the natives to reach the two strangers and their exhausted bodies were pulled into the boats. Back on the shore, the locals gathered, staring in wonder at the white skinned humans. They were mesmerised, most never having seen a white European before. It was not long before a large crowd had gathered around them. Once cared for and rehydrated in the shade of the trees, the two men started to regain their strength. Jacob and Jack became aware of their surroundings at the same time and as they registered the many sets of curious eyes which started at them, they naturally drew close to one another, concerned as to whether their rescuers where friend or foe.

Smiling, trying to look as friendly as possible Jacob was the first to speak,

"Hello, my name is Jacob, and this is Jack. Do any of you speak English?"

One of the tribe members with distinctive red markings on his face came forward and in broken English instructed the men to follow him.

Without waiting for a response, he walked away from the shoreline towards higher ground. The two men shakily rose to their feet and followed him, thanking their rescuers as they walked away by bowing their heads and motioning what they hoped to be a universal sign of gratitude with their hands in prayer position. Jacob and Jack wanted to ask questions as their red-faced guide took them through rough steep terrain, but they decided to remain silent. Ahead of them, as the ground flattened, appeared the most unexpected, beautiful sight imaginable, a palace.

Once inside the palace grounds, passing brightly coloured plants and flowers, the likes of which Jacob and Jack had never seen before, they reached the front entrance of the palace itself. Two guards stood to attention, one either side of the doors; the red-faced guide spoke to the guard on the left in a language undistinguishable to Jacob and Jack. One of the doors was opened from behind by a petit man, who invited the three of them inside. The palace was vast and filled with the sound of birds which were housed in delicate cages. The array of colours inside the palace was a feast for the eyes, brightly painted wood, the iridescent feathers of the birds and the beautiful local stone dazzled in the brightly lit rooms. Taking a left turn along a shorter corridor they entered a room which could only have been described as the gold room, the men mad never seen so much gold. At the far end were two large golden thrones, divided by a cage containing a pair of lovebirds. Both thrones were occupied, on the left sat a giant of man who it could only be assumed was the king and to his right a younger man, presumably his son.

"Welcome my friends!" boomed the elder of the pair, "I am King Zamora, and this is my son Prince Odin."

The king had a friendly demeanour and a perfect smile, Jacob and Jack felt immediately at ease in his presence. The prince smiled also but did not speak.

"You are from the broken ship?" King Zamora enquired.

"Yes," Jacob replied.

"So, tell me, what brings you to Guinea, I assume this was not your intended destination?"

The next hour was storytelling from both sides. Jacob and Jack were invited to join the king and prince for lunch, with conversation flowing, each man equally as fascinated to hear about the others lives.

"What's all the noise?" A new voice joined the conversation, a female.

"Ahh! Jacob and Jack let me introduce another member of my family, this is my daughter Princess Dina and her cousin Princess Aisha."

Jacob was the first to rise and bow his head to show respect for the beautiful young women being presented to him.

"Are you ladies joining us for lunch?" Jacob asked.

Princess Dina and Aisha giggled,

"We always eat together."

Dina sat at the chair that had been pulled back by the servant who stood in attendance just behind Jacob and Aisha sat down next to Jack. The table was laid with dishes the likes of which they had never seen before, a glorious tropical feast. Jacob and Jack ate until their bellies ached, delighted and very relieved to have met such wonderful, welcoming human beings.

The king stood, raised a goblet and announced in his

commanding voice,

"You two, are our new friends, you must stay here as my guests for as long as you wish, I insist."

Jacob and Jack looked at each other, and then back at the king. Nodding their heads, they accepted the generous offer with gratitude and rose from their seats to thank their hosts.

***

The palace was desirable both as a building of status and also for its valuable and precious contents. Numerous surrounding rival tribes, with varying degrees of success and on different occasions, had pushed the king's army to their limit, defending the grounds and all that lay within. Lookout towers around the perimeter of the palace complex and on-the-ground patrols were essential to the safety of all who lived within the palace walls.

Jacob showed much interest in the king's army, observing their training and tactics. He knew that his military skills could benefit them, and the king was only too delighted to take up Jacob's offer to assist in improving the security of the palace and the quality of the men's fighting skills. Every morning Jacob worked with the soldiers training them in the skills he had learned in the military back in England. The men lived closely with each other creating a good sense of camaraderie and were naturally disciplined. Their attitude and relationships meant they responded well to the new tactics implemented by Jacob and within a reasonably short space of time they became a professional defensive and offensive force, much like the English army and Jacob divided them into palace guards, regular infantry and elite warriors. The elite warriors were specially selected for night raids to free the prisoners from enemy tribes, both ordinary citizens and soldiers who had been captured over recent years. Such was the success of these operations that King Zamora called this group Jacob's Warriors.

Every day King Zamora consulted his shaman, a highly decorated man, festooned with bones and feathers, to Jacob he had an almost mythological look about him. The king always spoke with the shaman alone, but unknown to Jacob or Jack the shaman delivered dark messages. Every day since their arrival the shaman had had the same dream, warning him and his people that the presence of the white men was a bad omen for their future. The natives were also divided about the length of time the strangers were spending in their midst, while some idolised the king and trusted all that he did, others believed the white skinned men to be a bad omen also. King Zamora simply observed his guests and like all the people around him, could see that Jacob was pure of heart.

One day Prince Odin, his sister Dina and cousin Aisha invited Jacob and Jack on a safari trip which was to the include a visit to the forbidden and mysterious part of the kingdom that King Zamora was strongly against anyone visiting. Jacob and Jack graciously accepted the invitation, not knowing what dangers might lay in store for them, and the following day they started out on the three-day adventure into the jungle. Escorted by guards and accompanied by porters who carried all the provisions for the expedition, they ventured on foot through what seemed to be unexplored country. The scenery was breath-taking and the wildlife they encountered was such that they had never seen before.

They stopped at midday alongside an aquamarine coloured pool fed by a spectacular waterfall in which they took the opportunity to bathe and swim, before resting in the shade for a while and eating lunch. After their break, taken during the hottest part of the day, they ventured deeper into the jungle not aware that they were entering an area infested with cannibals. As dusk fell and the group prepared to make camp for the night, all of sudden the jungle became strangely quiet, and a feeling of dread took hold of them all.

The outer perimeter of their camp was manned by their guards who within moments vanished one by one, each slain by silent killers who then carried off their pray into the jungle, which grew ever darker by the minute. The remaining explorers were surrounded and helpless to defend themselves as they were ambushed by a second wave of cannibals, but Jack and Jacob somehow managed to escape the clutches of their captors and hid in horror, listening to the screams of Prince Odin and the princesses as they too were carried away. In the darkness the two men were powerless to do anything but resolved that at first light they would track the savages and rescue their friends.

Leaving a trail of pieces of clothing in their wake, in case someone might come looking for them, Jacob and Jack followed the footprints. Meanwhile one of the porters had also managed to escape unscathed and had made his way back to the palace to report what had happened to the king, who immediately rallied his elite warriors and supporting army, and set off to rescue his family.

Jacob and Jack journeyed for two days through hostile terrain until on the evening of the second day they heard noises ahead and realised that they were on the outskirts of the savages' settlement. They climbed a tree to get a good vantage point and assess their best course of action. At the centre of the settlement was a large fire on which decapitated bodies were being cooked. At first Jacob and Jack thought they were too late but closer inspection of the horrific scene revealed that the prince, princesses and some of the porters were in fact being held captive, tied to some trees on the periphery of the camp.

Jacob knew his only chance of helping his friends was to use the cover of nightfall, so he and Jack waited patiently until all but a few guards were asleep. At around midnight they silently crept out of their hiding place and stealthily around to the other side of the camp where their friends were imprisoned. The element of surprise served to their advantage as they overpowered the guards from behind, slitting their throats to silence each of them in one manoeuvre. The bloodied blades were then used to cut the ropes binding the prisoners' hands and feet, and with everyone freed the terrified group slipped silently away into the jungle, retreating as fast as they could back the way they came.

Not daring to rest, the exhausted group maintained a punishing pace as they escaped the nightmare that had befallen them and the terror of what could have been. Stumbling through the dark, with only the light of the moon and Jacob's trail to guide them, the silent escapees dared not look back to see if they were being followed. As the sun rose the next day the bedraggled companions were struggling to go on but were too afraid to rest so it was with enormous relief and jubilation that they met with King Zamora's army which was advancing to their rescue. The king's joy at being reunited with his son and daughter soon gave way to anger and the need for vengeance and with the rescue mission now complete the king ordered his men to be on the attack.

The savages, having discovered the escape of their prisoners, had immediately set out to recover their captives, not knowing that an army now awaited them. They stood no chance against the king's fighting force which, having dealt with the hunting party, then advanced to the savage's settlement and in a swift attack led by Jacob's Warriors, annihilated everyone they found.

Chapter Three – Africa, Virginia- 1768

It took time for the survivors of the cannibal attack to recover from their ordeal but when they were sufficiently well King Zamora declared a national holiday in the kingdom to celebrate the safe return of his son and daughter and in honour and recognition of the bravery of Jacob and Jack. Festivities went on throughout the day and as the sun lowered in the sky, the prince and princesses, together with Jacob and Jack, lit fires and torches around the palace grounds to welcome in the evenings celebrations.

"Here you go my brave ones," Dina said as she handed over a goblet of wine each to Jacob and Jack, "come and watch the dancing with me."

Drinks had been flowing all afternoon with servants always at hand to refill goblets, they had all lost count of how much they had had to drink.

Dina linked her arm with Jacob's to encourage him in the

direction of the stage. Most guests had already taken their seats waiting patiently for the king's family to take theirs, so the performance could begin. Aisha was already seated in the front row waiting for them.

"Perfect timing!" Aisha smiled as her friends took their places next to her.

Dancers burst on to the stage in an explosion of colour as the music began. Clapping and cheering from the audience almost drowned out the sound made by the musicians. On stage vibrant traditional dresses twirled, hips swung and coordinated hand movements mesmerised the delighted onlookers. To the right of the stage, between the performers and the audience, several children emulated the on-stage dancing. Dina, Jacob, Aisha and Jack joined in with the audience who were clapping their hands in time to the beating drums. More drinks were brought to them between performances, Jack joked that he had a magic refillable cup.

The next act was a snake charmer and this time the only sounds from the audience were gasps of wonder as the charmer used his pungi to bring the serpent forth from its basket. Fear amongst the audience was palpable as the powerful cobra's head moved from side to side, hypnotised by the music. Suddenly it's his hood flared, and Dina grabbed Jacob's hand for comfort, the effects of alcohol had removed any awkwardness between them, but their eyes remained fully focused on the snake, utterly transfixed. Later everyone rose from their seats applauding the snake charmer and his lethal sidekick. Jacob wandered backstage, interested in viewing the snake close up. Returning to the crowd he had been missed.

"Oh, there you are!" Dina exclaimed, "let's go and find the others," again she linked her arm with Jacob's.

"I think they went this way." Dina took the lead.

Making their way back inside the palace, they talked about the day's events and the night's performances, and before long it suddenly dawned on Jacob that they were approaching Dina's bedroom.

"Did you see Jack and Aisha come this way?" Jacob quizzed Dina.

"Mmm no, but I have something I was given today that I want to show you," Dina announced as she opened the door to her room. "Please sit down."

Dina ushered Jacob to sit on her bed while she poured wine into two goblets already positioned on her dressing table. Handing one to Jacob, she took a sip from her own. Dina returned to the dressing table, collected a highly decorated small box and went to sit next to Jacob on the bed.

"This is what I wanted to show you." Dina explained. Jacob looked at the box, then at Dina.

"It's a music box, shut your eyes."

Jacob did as he was asked. Instantly a delicate sound twinkled from the little box. It was like nothing he had ever heard before. The next thing he knew he felt the press of warm lips against his; with his eyes closed and reality blurred by the effects of alcohol, he believed the lips that were now kissing him belonged to Elizabeth. Dina kissed deeper, her tongue finding his as she loosened his clothing. The soft hands massaging Jacobs's chest felt like Elizabeth's. Reality, memory and imagination blended as Jacob and Dina's bodies entwined seeking and finding pleasure in each other.

Now lying side by side, Dina rested her head on Jacob's chest. Jacob looked at her long dark hair draped across his body. Utterly confused by alcohol and the night's events he drifted off to sleep. When he awoke early the next morning, Princess Dina was still asleep and fearful of the potential consequences of what they had done, Jacob quietly left her and returned to his own room.

Feeling a little worse for wear, Jacob drank water from a copper container, changed his clothes and then went for a walk around the palace grounds to clear his head. Tiny drops of dew on the flowers sparkled, nature's magic Jacob thought to himself. Returning to the palace, Jacob was apprehensive about facing the princess after their night together, anxious about how the easiness that had previously existed between them might have changed, but as he entered the building he need not have worried.

Jack, Dina and Aisha were preparing to go out, their faces aglow with the joy of a new day. Dina acted as though nothing at all unusual had happened the previous night, like it had all been just an illusion.

"Good morning Jacob, we are going to the market, would you like to come?" Dina asked, holding her leather pouch in her hand. Surprised by her nonchalance, Jacob could do nothing but agree to accompanying his friends.

At the market there was a noticeable change in the air, more noise and excitement than usual and a large crowd gathered in the centre.

"What's going on over there?" Princess Dina asked.

"Shall we take a look?" Aisha responded grabbing Dina's arm.

"Come on ladies," Jacob smiled as they all made their way over to join the crowd. The excitement had been caused by the arrival of a caravan of Arab traders. Friendly visitors were always welcome in the city and marketgoers were eager to see the new faces who brought with them new goods, new livestock and wealth to make purchases of local produce.

Princess Dina approached the traders to speak with the man who seemed to be in charge, he introduced himself as Ahmad from Jerusalem, and also his son whose name was Mustafa. Jacob, Jack and Aisha looked on and admired Dina's easy way with the strangers, they were having a very animated and friendly conversation with lots of gesturing.

As Dina returned to her friends she was smiling, her eyes wide with excitement.

"I have invited those charming gentlemen to join us this evening for dinner. My father is going to love them; they are so knowledgeable, with so many interesting stories to tell of their travels. I will send a guard to run ahead, so the kitchen can prepare."

By late afternoon preparations for a lavish feast were almost complete ahead of the arrival of the princess's guests. The traders had sent ahead a beautiful gift of an exquisitely carved stone statue depicting an Arabian horse and her foal which was given pride of place as the table centrepiece.

King Zamora was indeed delighted with his guests and wanted to know everything about their travels and the people they had met in different parts of the country. Delicacies the likes of which the traders had never before seen were brought up from the palace kitchens, as one course after another was served to the royal family and their guests. New friendships were firmly cemented and after a wonderful evening of food, wine and glorious stories Ahmad and his companions headed back to their camp.

Jacob had learned during the evening that the traders were not staying long in the city and would be returning home by ship at the end of the week. In bed that night, Jacob struggled to sleep. Whilst he had enjoyed the more than generous hospitality of the king, he could not shake the unease he had felt ever since the shipwreck, unease now so intense it dominated his every thought. Jacob loved the people who had taken him in, he loved the palace and everything about the city, but he knew this was not where he belonged, and he needed to continue the journey he had begun back in Liverpool. Whenever he had discussed these feelings with Jack, the only person he could share these thoughts with, Jack had also expressed his desire to return to England and to the family he had left behind.

Over the next few days Jacob and Jack secretly prepared for the departure they knew would be hard to make, but which was essential to their future happiness. The pair had spoken to Ahmad who was happy for them to join the caravan for the journey to the port. They had packed bags with supplies for their journeys and were committed to leaving the city when the Arab traders departed. On the day of their planned departure they went to speak to King Zamora and Prince Odin to explain why they had to leave. Neither the king nor the prince could argue with their reasons nor could they convince them to stay. The hardest part was going to be breaking the news to Dina and Aisha. The princesses were devastated when Jacob and Jack told them of their plans and fell into the arms of the men they had come to love, sobbing tearful farewells. It was with heavy hearts that the men pulled themselves away from Dina and Aisha and made their way to join the Arab traders who were packing up their tents and preparing to leave.

Within an hour Jacob and Jack were riding on camels alongside the Arab traders on their way to the main city port, each with their own memories of their time in the palace, memories that would stay with them for the rest of their lives. After days of journeying, a strong wind blew up seemingly out of nowhere, to cool the burning heat of the sun. Riding on high ground the train got their first glimpse of the sea and Mustafa told the men that they were approximately half a day away from the port. Their end goal now in sight, the caravan's pace quickened and soon they were starting the descent towards the main port.

The vegetation closer to the sea was denser and whilst beautiful to behold, it also provided ideal hiding places for the bandits who lurked on the outskirts of the port city, lying in wait to pray on unsuspecting travellers coming to and from the docks.

Jacob was admiring the view and taking a gulp of water from his leather bottle, when the man on the camel in front of him suddenly fell from his mount, with an arrow jutting out of his neck, a moment later another man to his side was also hit and slid to the ground. Jacob instinctively took charge of the situation, shouting instructions to his fellow travellers to brandish the weapons they all carried and to charge the camels at their assailants, who by now had emerged from the bushes wielding large blades, and slashing indiscriminately at the camels and their riders. In the chaos of the attack Jacob spied a bandit coming up behind Mustafa. Leaping from his camel Jacob landed on the back of the would-be attacker and in one swift move slit his throat. All around the bandits were being defeated by the Arabs who over the years had learned to protect themselves from such attacks, but it was Jacob's military expertise and quick thinking which had first galvanised the group when faced with the surprise onslaught. A few remaining assailants, seeing their cause was lost, retreated into the cover of the jungle leaving those who had survived the attack surveying the damage, grateful to be alive. Jack was wounded, a large gash on his leg oozing blood and becoming more and more painful as his adrenaline started to subside. Jacob pulled some cloth from his saddle bag and wrapped it tightly around Jack's bloody leg to create a tourniquet.

Ahmad, Mustafa and the remaining company of traders were in awe of Jacob's skills, each of them aware that they owed their lives to his quick thinking. Fearful of lingering too long, knowing they might not withstand a second attack, the group quietly and respectfully loaded their dead onto one of the wagons and went on their way. It was a sombre procession of men, each having been faced with their own mortality, which journeyed the final leg to the docks. As they rode in Ahmed pulled up alongside Jacob and removing a gold ring from a finger on his left hand he presented it to Jacob.

"This is for you my friend, to show my appreciation. You saved the life of my son and for that I will forever be your debt." Jacob looked at the ring, noticing the traders initial etched in the stone. "Everyone knows Ahmad, just show this ring and you will have help wherever you go."

"I will treasure it always," said Jacob, overwhelmed by the very personal gift.

Mustafa appeared alongside his father.

"My wife is expecting our first child very soon, if it is a boy, we shall name him Jacob to show my appreciation to you for saving my life." He smiled his gratitude and rode on in silence, contemplating what could have been.

"That truly is an honour Mustafa," Jacob replied.

A cacophony of sounds, sights and smells unique to seaports met the travel-weary caravan as they lumbered into the dockside, hugely relieved at being off the road. Ships of varying sizes waited expectantly in the water, Jacob noticed the most common cargo seemed to be slaves. The Arab traders located their own ship and were greeted by their crew, who busied themselves loading goods and supplies on board.

The time had come for Jack and Jacob to say goodbye. Jacob gave a letter to Jack and asked him to hand deliver it to his brother Michael, in it he told Michael briefly of his sojourn in Africa and his intention now to continue on to America as planned. He also asked Michael to take care of Jack and ensure that he was found a good job as reward for saving his life. They said goodbye to each other, wishing each other luck and then went their separate ways in search of ships which would take them on the next stage of their journeys.

Jacob approached the largest of the ships, having been told by Ahmad's crew that it was heading to Virginia. He spoke briefly to the ship's captain, securing himself a job on board the slave trade ship, one of the many Guineaman ships trafficking slaves from one continent to another. Once on board, he worked hard, keeping himself to himself by choosing to have little conversation with the others. Days turned into weeks, the weather was kind and seas calm.

Jacob found it impossible to remain silent about the treatment of the slaves on board the ship. He regularly argued with crew members for withholding food from the slaves and witnessed slaves beaten for the slightest misdemeanour. He knew some of the slaves had been raped but he was powerless to do anything about it. In the eyes of the traders, the slaves were no longer humans with their own thoughts and feelings, they were merely commodities.

Death and disease were rife on board the Guineaman ship. Dysentery, dehydration and a lack of any kind of sanitation claimed the lives of some of the crew, but it was the human cargo who were impacted in greater numbers, perishing in overcrowded cramped conditions, chained to their plank beds. Jacob witnessed the misery of these poor souls and it weighed heavily on him. Day by day he was becoming more and more consumed by a terrible sadness which threatened to engulf him. He longed for the day when they would reach land and he could leave the hell in which he had found himself.

***

Although it had been many months since Adam Adelson had received a letter telling him to one day expect the arrival of his second cousin Jacob, he still went to the harbour whenever a ship was coming in from overseas, in case, per chance, one day the ship would be carrying his runaway relative.

For six long weeks Jacob had been at sea, a voyage that had seemed to go on forever and his feelings when he stepped on to dry land were beyond words. It had been so long since he had set out from Liverpool that he held out very little hope that his cousin would still be expecting him, so it was with enormous relief that he spied a man on the docks who could only be Adam Adelson.

The well-dressed gentleman approached Jacob.

"Welcome to Virginia, you must be Jacob!"

"Yes, Yes, I am." Jacob responded, suddenly very conscious of his appearance and how dreadful he must smell.

"Your brother Michael explained everything that happened to you and your beloved wife Elizabeth. I'm so, so sorry for your loss and all that you have been through."

Jacob's eyes filled with tears. He simply shook his head and looked down towards his feet.

"There is plenty of time for explanations, here let's get you to the house, I can't imagine what a time you've had."

Adam showed Jacob to the waiting carriage. Two hours later the men arrived at a large white house covered in creeping flowering vines.

Disembarking the carriage Adam extended is arm in the direction of the beautiful building ahead of them.

"Welcome to Berkeley House," he said.

The household had obviously seen them approach and were now gathered in the shade of the front porch. Of all the people waiting outside the house to welcome Jacob, he was particularly taken with a striking young woman with eyes the colour of sapphires and beautiful brown hair which cascaded in ringlets over her shoulders and down her back. She was introduced to him as Abby, Adams daughter.

Adam Adelson was a kind-hearted man of honour. He owned a plantation worked by men and women who had been sold to him as slaves but to whom he paid wages and treated fairly. Jacob welcomed the opportunity to help Adam with the running of the plantation and immersed himself in his new life in Virginia. Within a year he was married to Adam's daughter Abby and soon after their twins Joseph and Rebecca were born.

Chapter Four - Africa - 1780

It was now twelve years since Jacob and Jack had left Africa, but they had not been forgotten. Nine months after their departure, Princess Dina had given birth to Jacob's son Benjamin and within a few days, Aisha had also given birth to a baby girl who she named Lulu meaning 'pearl', a gift left behind by Jack. The cousins had been bereft after the departure of the men they had grown to love so they were both wonderfully surprised when they learned they were each carrying their children. Lulu and Benjamin grew up side by side, going everywhere and doing everything together. The sound of their running feet and laughter echoed in the palace corridors and they brought joy to all who knew them. Princess Dina and Aisha were also together daily, offering love and support to each other as still their hearts ached for the fathers of their respective children.

Rumours of unrest on the borders of the kingdom reached the palace and King Zamora was forced to send many of his warriors and palace guards off to defend his people from invasion by neighbouring tribes. It left the palace woefully unprotected.

One evening strong winds swept in, tearing at the branches of trees in the palace grounds. From the dining room of the palace Princess Dina could hear the stabled horses, clearly agitated by the gales and she looked out of the window, concerned by their unusual behaviour regardless of the unusual weather. She was even more surprised when suddenly the horses burst out of the stables, bolting in different directions. It was then that she heard a commotion within the palace which caused her heart to race. Running from the dining room, Dina could hear shouting, screaming and the sound of many feet rushing through the palace. Her first thought was Benjamin but as she tried to make her way through the main hall and up the grand staircase to the upper floor, she encountered a group of men she had never seen before, men who were armed and who were clearly intent on no good.

Indeed, the men were slavers, accompanied by tribesmen from a neighbouring enemy tribe, driven by greed and envy. The attackers seemed to have blown in with the winds and were intent on causing as much disruption as possible, sweeping the palace clean of all valuables and taking prisoner all who inhabited the once impenetrable citadel. Dina doubled back on herself to try to flee, but the attackers had infiltrated all areas and she was captured as she headed for another staircase to try and get to her son. Dina's captor tied her hands behind her back with rope, she could smell the stench of sweat and grime on his body as he went about the task. Pushing her roughly he forced her down a corridor which led to her father's study and as she stumbled forward she caught a glimpse of a body slumped on the floor. Horror-struck Dina screamed for her father, managing to escape her captors and rushing over to kneel next to his lifeless body.

"Father, father," Dina wailed, beside herself with anguish, tears streaming down her face.

Her captors had no time for sentiment, grabbing her roughly by the arms and pulling her to her feet.

"Move" one of them snarled, gripping her arm and shoving her away further down the corridor as she tried to turn her head for one last look at her beloved father.

In a daze and numb with grief Dina was taken to where more and more captives were being brought together, all with their hands bound, all equally shocked at the suddenness of the attack and fearful for what was to become of them. Through her tears Dina saw that Odin, Aisha, Lulu and Benjamin had also been captured and when they saw her distress, their worst fears were confirmed.

"Where's father?" asked Odin.

Dina looked at him, hardly able to speak the words she knew she had to say.

"Dina, where's father?" Odin repeated.
"He's gone," was all Dina managed to reply, not wanting to speak the terrible truth, saying it out loud would make it real.

"Gone where?" Odin asked, fearing the answer.

"Gone…, Odin…, father is dead!" Between sobs Dina confirmed Odin's worst fears. Unable to embrace her brother Dina simply rested her head on his shoulder, as Odin bravely swallowed his own tears. He was king now, he could not allow his subjects to see his emotion, even though all around him is newly acquired kingdom was being destroyed and his people enslaved.

When all of the palace's inhabitants had been rounded up and bound they were forced to spend the night on the floor of the main hall. With the kingdom's army and warriors away protecting outer borders, an unexpected enemy had attacked and caught the palace unawares and unprepared. They had been easy prey, sitting ducks. The captives knew there was no chance of escape and no chance of rescue, their fates now lay in the hands of their captors and in their hearts, they knew that meant that they were most likely headed for a life of slavery.

Chapter Five - London - 1781

Major Henry Clive spent most of his evenings drinking and gambling, and tonight was no exception. Dressed in military uniform, as was his wont, he barked orders to his household staff as he prepared to leave to attend a gaming night at the home of a fellow officer of the East India Company.

Clutching a partially drunk bottle of red wine, Henry climbed into his waiting carriage and proceeded to further empty the bottle as the horses trotted off in the rapidly fading early evening light. Nearing the end of the journey the carriage came to an abrupt halt, barely a mile from its destination. The driver appeared at the carriage window.

"The front horse has lost a shoe sir," he explained.

"Oh! For God's sake you bloody useless man." Henry growled as he exited the carriage.

Steadying himself he pointed roughly in the direction of the host's property.

"I will walk," Henry shouted angrily, swaying from side to side along the uneven road, gripping tightly to his almost-empty bottle, the Autumn leaves crunching beneath his boots. As the house came into view, Henry was suddenly aware of the sound of horses hooves behind him. Unable to see anything other than the partially illuminated house ahead of him, Henry turned around and waved his arms to alert the approaching carriage of his presence on the road in the hope of getting a lift for the remainder of the journey.

"Room for one more?" he shouted into the blackness, the sound of hooves getting louder.

Inebriated, not fully appreciating the lack of visibility and misjudging the speed at which the carriage was travelling, Henry stepped right in to the path of the galloping horses. The impact knocked him off his feet forcing him to the ground and under the carriage wheels. The accident seemed to happen in slow motion as the carriage tipped on to its side with the sound of cracking wood and screams from the passengers within, filling the night air, but Major Henry Clive witnessed none of what happened next as his battered body lay still in the darkness.

***

The accident had left the major bedridden with injuries

from which he would never recover. A daily visitor to him was Alistair Stafford, who was paranoid that knowing the end was near and possibly needing to confess his sins, Henry might reveal the truth about Elizabeth's death. Alistair's visits were always brief, with Alistair usually talking about himself, and only intermittent grunts of acknowledgement from Henry. Although he did not discuss it with Henry, Alistair had deep concerns that Henry would divulge the many dark secrets they shared. He hoped fervently that every evil act they had committed together would be buried along with Henry when the time came. When Henry was gone the only person left to eliminate would be Jacob Goldsmith and Alistair would not rest until Jacob had been silenced.

The week following the accident, Henry's condition was worsening rather than improving. Externally he looked merely bruised, albeit badly so, but internally his ribs were broken, and his lungs and other vital organs were severely damaged. Henry knew he was dying and called for Michael, Jacob's brother, to bring David over to see him. David was now a mature young man of sixteen years old.

David had no idea why he was being brought to see this dying man but politely did as he was bid and was met at Henry's house by Alistair and his son Stan, who escorted him in to Henry's bedroom. Henry asked David to sit on the bed and handed him the cult's all-seeing eye necklace.

"This is for you," Henry whispered. David looked at the necklace in his hand briefly and then back to Henry.

"Why me?" he asked.

"Jacob is not your father David," said Henry softly.

"What? What do you mean? I don't understand," responded a confused David.

"I am your father." Henry confessed.

Speechless, David stared at Henry disbelief, a thousand questions suddenly swirling around his head, but the questions would have to wait as Henry closed his eyes and slipped again into sleep, seemingly exhausted from the effort of talking.

David's questions however would never be answered. At least not by his father.

Later that day Major Henry Clive's chest rose and fell for the last time.

Chapter Six – Virginia, America - 1790

Jacob's twins Joseph and Rebecca were nearing adulthood and Jacob was content with the life he had made for himself at Berkeley House. The plantation, despite uniquely paying the wages of its workers, was will hugely profitable and life was good. Most days Jacob and Adam would ride out together, checking the land and speaking with the workers. Adam handed more and more responsibility to his son-in-law making the plantation very much a family business.

Whenever he could Jacob took the opportunity to pursue charitable work to help slaves in other cities. As always Jacob was kind and respectful to his fellow man.

One morning Jacob and Adam had been out riding for several hours and reached the outermost boundary of the plantation. Both men were relaxed, their reins hanging loose in their hands as the track narrowed and Jacob moved from beside Adam to ride in front of him. Suddenly a rattlesnake appeared on the track ahead of Jacob causing his horse to rear onto its hind legs and throw Jacob to the ground. Jacob hit the ground hard, every bit of air pushed from his lungs, his left shoulder throbbing having taken most of the impact. The rider-less horse galloped away through the crops, trampling a new path through the plants.

Adam was off his horse in a moment.

"Jacob, are you alright?" he asked, holding tightly to his own horse's reins for fear he too would flee.

Unable to catch his breath Jacob groaned.

A young worker had witnessed the entire unfortunate episode and had immediately run from the field to assist his masters in whatever way he could, waving a long stick at the snake until it disappeared into the undergrowth. He knelt down beside Jacob anxious to help.

"Let's get him up onto my horse," Adam instructed the young man and with Jacob's face contorted in pain from the injury to his shoulder, Adam and the boy managed to get Jacob up and on the saddle. The worker led Jacob back to Berkeley House while Adam went to retrieve Jacob's mount. Ordinarily Jacob would have engaged in conversation with the boy, but the pain was too intense. When they arrived back at the house the boy held on to the horse while staff helped Jacob to dismount and then took him inside.

"Wait downstairs for me," Jacob instructed the young worker as he was led away, "I wish to thank you properly."
The boy left the staff helping Jacob while he went off to locate the stables and having returned Adam's horse to the care of the grooms he went back to house and waited on the porch as instructed. A short while later Jacob appeared with colour back in his cheeks and invited the boy into the house.

"Come in, and take a seat," Jacob gestured to an exquisitely carved chair with satin upholstery as they entered the drawing room.

Most slaves would have felt uneasy and out of place in such surroundings, but this boy seemed nonplussed by the luxury of the house.

"I am Jacob, what is your name?"

"It is Benjamin, sir."

"I appreciate your kindness and bravery Benjamin." Jacob extended his right arm to shake Benjamin's hand. Both men smiled. There was something familiar about the boy whose skin was not as dark as the other workers on the plantation.

Jacob made an instant decision.

"I need help with this house Benjamin, we require

someone to assist with general maintenance. You will earn more than you get working on the plantation and there will be a room for you in the servants quarters if you are interested?"

Benjamin's face lit up at the prospect of no longer working in the fields.

"Thank you, sir, I would be honoured to work for you here at the house," Benjamin replied.

Benjamin worked hard in his new role, was quick to learn and gained a variety of new skills. Late one afternoon Benjamin returned to the original field he had worked. His small cart contained some tools which he had repaired, ready to be used again by his friends, family and other workers. Benjamin had finished his work at the house and was excited to see his mother Dina, aunt Aisha and cousin Lulu, he slapped the reins on the horse's rump to encourage a slightly faster pace. Benjamin's excitement turned to dismay as he approached the fields in which his family worked and saw his mother resting on a blanket in the shade of a large tree. Dina was clutching her stomach, sweating and groaning, she looked up when she heard his voice.

"Mother, mother what's wrong?" Benjamin shouted as he ran to kneel beside her. Dina grabbed her son's hand.

"The pain darling, my stomach, argh!" her face distorted from the agony, "I need help, Benjamin."

Placing his strong arms under his mother's shoulders and knees, Benjamin carefully lifted her onto the back of the cart and once assured that she was as comfortable as she could be he steered the horse back to Berkeley House.

On arrival, Benjamin carried Dina into the servant's quarters and placed her on his bed, then he ran to find Jacob who was working in the study.

"Sir, I need your help please," Benjamin implored.

"What is wrong Benjamin?" enquired Jacob, concerned for the boy who was clearly very distressed.

"It's my mother, she is sick."

Jacob rang a bell to alert a member of staff. A maid appeared within seconds,

"Martha, I need you to fetch Doctor Preston as quickly as you can please."

"Yes sir." Martha replied, turning on her heels and rushing from the room to the plantation infirmary which Adam had insisted on establishing to care for his many workers.

Jacob followed Benjamin to his room, not for one moment expecting that Benjamin's mother would be none other than Princess Dina.

"Good God!" Jacob exclaimed, utterly flabbergasted when he saw who was lying on the bed.

"Jacob?" queried Dina, a mixture of shock and pain on her face.

"What are you doing here?" Jacob asked rushing to Dina's bedside and embracing her. "I didn't expect to ever see you again."

"Mother, what's going on, how do you two know each other?" Benjamin enquired, confused and concerned all at the same time.

At that moment Doctor Preston arrived and burst in to the room.

"Gentlemen, please allow me to deal with the patient."

Jacob and Benjamin made way to allow the doctor to examine his patient as they looked at each with confusion on both their faces.

Jacob watched on as though in a dream as the doctor assisted Dina while Benjamin held her hand. When the doctor was satisfied that it was nothing serious, he made sure Dina was comfortable then bade farewell to the three of them, promising to return the following day.

Once he was gone Benjamin immediately turned to Jacob.

"Sir, how do you know my mother?"

"Princess Dina is your mother?" questioned Jacob, the disbelief evident in his voice.

"Well yes," Benjamin replied, "we were captured by slave traders at our palace in Guinea and brought here to work."

Dina interrupted them holding out her hand to Jacob who went to sit next to her again on the bed,

"Oh Jacob, I can't believe it's you. I never thought I would have the opportunity to tell you this, either of you."

Dina looked from one to the other, Benjamin on one side of the bed holding one hand and Jacob on the other. Taking a deep breath, she revealed the truth to them both,

"Jacob, this is your son. Benjamin, this is your father."

It took a few moments for the words to sink in for both father and son.

"But how mother? How can Jacob be my father?" asked Benjamin in disbelief.

Through tears of joy at being reunited, Dina and Jacob explained to Benjamin how they had come to know each other, then Dina and Benjamin told Jacob the horrific tale of how they had been captured and brought to Virginia. Jacob was elated to learn that he had another son, especially such a fine young man as Benjamin, but he was also dismayed and angry to learn of all they had been through and terribly sad to learn of King Zamora's death.

Dina explained how their capturers had split their group between two plantations, one in Virginia and one in Georgia. Prince Odin had been sent to work at a plantation in Georgia and they had not been able to communicate at all since leaving the ship. When she told Jacob that Aisha and Jack's daughter Lulu were also working on his plantation, Jacob had them sent for immediately and there were more emotional reunions.

Leaving Aisha, Benjamin and Lulu to take care of Dina, Jacob went to find his wife, it was only fair that she should hear this news from him. Long ago Jacob had told Abby all about his past in both London and Africa. He had confessed to the fact that his friendship with Dina had strayed one night to something more, but he had never imagined that a child had been conceived. Abby listened quietly and thoughtfully as he relayed to her his discovery that he had another son and that his son was in fact Benjamin, who was by now a well-known and popular character around the house and the plantation. She could see her husband's delight in what he had learned that day and shared in his happiness. When Jacob continued with his story about Dina, Aisha, Lulu and Prince Odin, her heart went out to them for all that they had suffered.

When the rest of the family were gathered together they listened incredulous as Jacob relayed the story. Joseph and Rebecca were thrilled to find they had another brother, they had come to know Benjamin well since he had started working at the house and already thought of him as part of the family. Despite the unusual situation they all found themselves in, everyone wanted to make things work, feeling blessed to have found each other.

Adam assured Dina, Aisha, Benjamin and Lulu that they would no longer be working on the plantation and they were now to consider themselves his guests, although Benjamin insisted that he continue with his job in return for Adam's kind hospitality. Adam also gifted to them one of the plantation houses with their own staff, as befitted members of a royal family. Virginia would never be home to them, but Adam made it as comfortable for them as he possibly could and for that Dina was eternally grateful.

Meanwhile, Jacob was determined to find Prince Odin to reunite him with his sister and wrote to the owners of each of the plantations in Georgia. Months passed with no news until one day he received the letter he had hoped for. Prince Odin had been located, along with his wife and three children.

Jacob was elated to receive the letter and immediately headed over to Dina's house. Dina was in the garden upon Jacob's arrival and smiled as he walked down the path waving the letter above his head.

"Dina! Dina! I've got such good news!"

"What news?" she called back.
"Read this."

Jacob passed the letter to Dina. Jacob stared at her patiently while she read, waiting for the contents of the letter to register.

"You did it, you found him?"

Tears of joy rolled down her cheeks.

"Yes, I have, and I want you to help me with their new home," Jacob gestured to an empty property only yards from Dina's home.

"Is this real Jacob? Do you mean my brother will be my new neighbour?"

"Indeed, now come on we've got lots to do. A carriage has already been sent to collect them all."

Princess Dina could not have been happier, she had missed her brother terribly. With the help of everyone, she set about creating a beautiful home for him and the new family she was yet to meet.

Chapter Seven- London, Virginia, Jerusalem, Bombay and Tibet - 1792

Elizabeth's children, David and Sarah, had long desired to be reunited with their father in America. Their Uncle Michael had been the best possible guardian, loving them as if they were his own, raising them alongside his son Daniel.

Since the death of Henry and the revelation that he was David's real father, David had been groomed by Alistair Stafford and trained to become a fully-fledged member of the cult which, unknown to him, had claimed the life of his mother. David had been drawn in to the darkness and had worn the all-seeing eye necklace every day since the night Henry had died.

Alistair told David that he had some business in Virginia on behalf of the East India Company and that he would be accompanying them on their trip, so together Alistair, David and Sarah set off on the long sea voyage. Prior to the trip, Alistair had told his son Stan that if he did not return then he should know that Jacob Goldsmith had something to do with it.

***

On arrival at the port in Virginia, Sarah, David and Alistair found accommodation for the night. The next morning as David and Sarah arranged transport to the plantation, Alistair asked David for the location of Jacob's home, telling him that he would try and follow on later once his business was done. David had no idea of course that Alistair's sole purpose for coming to Virginia was to silence Jacob forever.

As Sarah and David journeyed to the plantation through the Virginian countryside, Sarah was captivated by all the unfamiliar sights, sounds and smells, but David was lost in his own thoughts, imagining, as he had so often, what it would be like to tell Jacob the harsh truth of his parentage.

Jacob was working in his study when he heard a horse and carriage approach and looked out of the window, but he did not recognise the handsome young couple who stepped out and approached the front door of the house.

The siblings were greeted at the door by a maid who showed them into the house, then went to find Abby to let her know that Jacob's son and daughter from England were waiting for him in the parlour. Abby could hardly contain her excitement, knowing what it would mean to her husband to see his children again, and rushed upstairs to find him in his study.

"Darling, your children from England are here, here in the parlour, they've come to see you."

Jacob could hardly comprehend Abby's words, not knowing what to say or how to respond to the news. They had been so young when he last saw them and had been through so much, losing their mother in such horrific circumstances and then their father too. Jacob was struck by a gamut of emotions as he followed his wife downstairs and nervously entered the room.

Despite the years apart, when face-to-face with each other Jacob knew his children immediately. The well-dressed young man with an unusual necklace, a disturbing memory from Jacob's past, and a beautiful blonde girl, the image of her mother. The reunion was emotional as one would expect, embracing one another and not wanting to let go, it hardly seemed real to Jacob to have his children in the room with him after so many years apart.

Jacob wanted to know everything, all about their lives and about the family back home in England. David and Sarah spoke about their memories of their mother, about growing up with their uncle and also of their journey to America. At times during their conversation Jacob struggled to stay focused as memories of the past came back to haunt him and questions swirled around his head like leaves in a storm.

By the end of the day all the family had been introduced to David and Sarah, including Dina, Aisha, Benjamin and Lulu. It was an extraordinary gathering that congregated around the dinner table that night, as half-siblings had the chance to get to know each other and Jacob looked on, still in disbelief at having all five of his children in the same room.

It was past midnight when everyone retired, rooms had been prepared for Sarah and David who were completely exhausted from the day's events and their long journey to get there. Abby held her husband's hand as they mounted the stairs together to their bedroom, each lost in their own thoughts and the events of the day.

"Good night sweetheart," were the last words Jacob heard before he slipped into a restless slumber.

Elizabeth occupied Jacob's dreams that night, visions of her mutilated body and her voice screaming his name, begging him to rescue her. It was a dream he had not had for some time but one which had reoccurred frequently in the years after her tragic death.

***

The next morning conversation around the breakfast table continued where it had left off the night before, but Jacob had little appetite and sat quietly listening to everyone else, hardly contributing at all to the animated discussions. His Virginia family had warmly welcomed David and Sarah in to their fold and as they talked amongst themselves it was almost as if they had all grown up together, not thousands of miles apart. Jacob's joy however, at being reunited with his children, was tainted by the stirring up of old memories and a pain, long suppressed, which had resurfaced.

***

One rain drenched Sunday evening, two weeks after the arrival of David and Sarah, Jacob called in to see Princess Dina, Lulu, Aisha and Benjamin. Part social call, part business, Jacob had tea with all of them before heading back to Berkeley House. Having said his goodbyes, Jacob closed the door and once outside, pulled his coat over his head to shield himself from the downpour. Meanwhile, after bidding farewell to his father, Benjamin spotted Jacob's money bag on the hallway dresser.

Grabbing the bag, Benjamin ran from the house in pursuit of his father, hoping to catch up with him. Within moments he was soaked to the skin from the torrential rain but spotting his father up ahead he proceeded to follow him. Out of nowhere there suddenly appeared a second figure, a shadowy presence, dressed all in black, also following Jacob. The figure seemed unaware that he was being observed, intent only on closing in on Jacob. It was then that Benjamin saw the figure raise his arm, his hand clutching a knife.

Calling out to his father, Benjamin sprinted forward, with speed he did not know he was capable of and hurtling himself at Jacob's assailant he leapt on to this back, grabbing him around his neck. The force of Benjamin launching himself at Jacob's attacker knocked them both to the ground.

Struggling to make sense of the scene unfolding before him, it took Jacob a moment to recognise Alistair as he thrashed around in the mud with Benjamin who was attempting to wrestle the knife from Alistair's hand. Blinded by the lashing rain, Jacob ran over to help and noticed blood pouring from Alistair's leg. In the struggle with Benjamin, Alistair had somehow himself been stabbed by his own poisoned blade, a blade whose intended victim was Jacob. Alistair writhed in pain, having released the blade to Benjamin, and clamped both his hands around his wounded thigh, trying to stem the flow of blood, but the poison was rapidly infiltrating his veins and he knew he was dying.

Jacob and Benjamin knelt down beside Alistair, Jacob needed to know why this man had tried to kill him. He leaned in close to Alistair's ashen face.

"What are you doing here? Why did you try to kill me?"

There was a pause as Alistair lifted his arm, wiped his brow with the back of his hand, and with dark evil eyes stared intensely and directly at Jacob.

Alistair mumbled four words. Jacob looked at Benjamin, who was kneeling the other side of Alistair.

"I didn't hear what he said father, did you?"

Jacob shook his head and through gritted teeth, grabbed Alistair's shoulders and shook him.

"Tell me. Tell me now, what did you say?" Jacob shuffled on his knees closer to Alistair and placed his right ear close to his mouth.

"Tell me," Jacob yelled with urgency, seeing the life ebbing away from his assailant.

Coughing and spluttering, with saliva spraying from his mouth, Alistair whispered,

"I killed your wife."

Jacob grabbed the collar of Alistair's cloak and pulled him closer, as Alistair struggled for breath.

"What do you mean you killed my wife, why?"

Alistair, a hairs breath from death, and nose to nose with Jacob, had a twisted grin etched upon his face.

"David is not your son, he was Henry's." The revelation was like a knife to Jacob's heart.

"What?" was all he could manage to say.

"I. Killed. Elizabeth." Alistair's final words.

Jacob shoved Alistair's limp body back on to the sodden ground and looked up to see Benjamin watching on confused as to who this man was and why he would want to kill his father.
"Are you hurt?" Jacob asked.

"A bit bruised I think, but who is this man father? Why was he trying to kill you? What did he say to you?" Benjamin winced as he clambered to his feet, slipping in the mud.

"Come on, let us get you home," said Jacob, as he placed Benjamin's arm over and around his neck providing support.

"But what about him? Who is he? Do you know him? Why was he trying to kill you?" Benjamin nodded towards Alistair's lifeless body.

"So many questions. Let's see to you first, he's dead anyway."

Benjamin, surprised at his father's reaction, clung to Jacob as they stumbled towards Berkeley House.

It was Abby who opened the door to the bedraggled pair and was dismayed to see that their clothes were bloodstained as well as soaking wet and muddy.

"Oh, my goodness darling, whatever happened? Are you hurt, Benjamin are you hurt, whose blood is that?" she fired questions at them both as wearily they entered the house and began to peel off their sodden clothes.

"Attacked," were the only words to pass Jacob's lips.

"Who, you? You were attacked?"

"Yes, Benjamin saved me."

With a sharp intake of breath Abby responded,

"Are you alright? Did they hurt you?"

"There was only one man darling, Benjamin overpowered him."

Abby's eyes widened as her right hand covered her mouth.

"What, what did he want?"

"Money perhaps, I don't know. Let's be grateful that Benjamin came after me and managed to stop him."

Realising that Jacob clearly did not wish to discuss the matter further, Abby respected her husband's wish to end the conversation. Tugging at his clothing, she looked into his eyes, searching for answers, but found none.

"Come on, let's get you out of these wet clothes."

A small puddle had formed under Jacob and Benjamin's drenched and mud-soaked bodies.

"You can tell me all about it tomorrow darling."

***

The night was full of terrors for Jacob as sleep eluded him. Over and over in his mind he replayed the attack and the shocking confession that had followed. When he closed his eyes Jacob could see Elizabeth's mutilated body lying on their bed, a baby who looked like Henry Clive, and Henry himself with that knowing smile of his and that necklace he had always worn, the one which now hung around David's neck.

The next day Jacob was still in turmoil, wondering if he should tell David about Alistair's confession. He was now seeing David through different eyes, seeing the similarities between him and Henry, the black hair and a certain brooding demeanour, but David was also so like Elizabeth. No matter how hard he looked, Jacob could see nothing of himself in the boy. In his heart he had always known that something was amiss after David's birth, the way Elizabeth had grown so distant from him but then, after she had been murdered, his life had been thrown into chaos and it had been so long since he had seen his children that in reality he hardly knew them at all.

Jacob was not to know that all the while the secret he thought he was keeping was already known to David, who out of choice had maintained the charade for his own benefit. He did not wish to sully the good name of his mother, who to so many people had been a saint. Despite all that had happened, she was still extremely well respected in society and status in society was extremely important to David.

***

Life went on in Virginia with David and Sarah settling there and making it their home. There were many celebrations, festivals, birthdays, weddings and charity events, and the tobacco business went from strength to strength keeping the Adelsons and Goldsmiths extremely busy. Of course, life also threw its challenges their way, but between them they shared the good times as well as overcoming the bad.

It was a joy to all when Benjamin and Lulu realised that their lifelong friendship had turned to the deepest of love. They were married in the gardens of Berkeley House and within the year had produced twin boys. Jacob, Dina and Aisha relished their new roles as grandparents, Abby too adored the new additions to the ever-expanding family.

The one person who often appeared disengaged when all the family were together, and at times a mere observer, was David. Night time was when David felt alive. He would go off for days at a time, saying that he was meeting and staying with friends but all the while he was attending secret cult meetings in various locations. Where ever he went his all-seeing-eye necklace was a sign to all those who knew to look for it, to others it was merely an unusual piece of jewellery.

Eventually David tired of life in Virginia, finding it too restrictive. His lifestyle choices and the promise of higher status within the cult led him to pursue a new life in New York. Anonymity was easier in the big city and he became more and more involved in cult activities, falling deeper and deeper into the darkness it represented. The sect he belonged to grew in numbers until the day came that David was to be ordained as its high priest.

Hundreds of hooded cult members gathered for the ceremony with the statue of the Goddess Jinn their focal point. For some of the newer members this would be the first time they had experienced a ritual sacrifice and the heightened anticipation and excitement in the room was palpable. David approached the Goddess with his black hooded robe partially covering his face. Tied to the altar a young goat bleated and tugged to try and free itself from the rope around its neck. Its hooves dancing as though treading on hot coals. All eyes were on David as the sound of chanting and the rhythmic beating of the ritual drum filled the night air.

Just like his father before him all those years ago in Bombay, David performed the ritual sacrifice then raised his blood-stained hands to the Goddess in reverence to her wants and needs. As he did so his hooded cloak fell open to reveal to onlookers the all-seeing eye necklace.

Having reached the pinnacle of his career within the cult, and having spent a year living in New York, David was beginning to feel disenchanted. The choices he had once made seemed to him to have been the wrong ones and without his loving family around him and only cult members for company he began to feel empty inside. The darkness of the cult was starting to take its toll on him and the realisation that perhaps he had walked the wrong path started to occupy his thoughts more and more every day.

Spring came, announced by the resurgence of new life on trees and in the hedgerows of parks and gardens. Where once David would not have appreciated the season of new beginnings, this time it resonated strongly with him and he reflected further on the life he was leading. The cult no longer held the draw for him that it once had. He began to realise that perhaps there was more of his mother in him than he had previously thought and that he could turn his back on the darkness. He became determined that, unlike his father, he could walk away from the cult towards the light and a path of righteousness. Recalling the charitable work that his mother was remembered for, he made the conscious decision to strive to be more like her and follow her example rather than that of the father he had never really known.

With this revelation, David's desire to cleanse and purge himself of past misdemeanours became his primary concern and the best way he knew of doing this was to renounce his current way of life, give up his possessions and begin the process of becoming a monk. Within hours of making this life-changing decision, David penned a letter to Jacob explaining that he had decided to journey to Tibet to realise his intentions.

***

For the Adelsons and Goldsmiths of Virginia, life continued to provide health, wealth and happiness. Jacob was surprised to receive David's letter, but it was clear from the contents that David was sincere and most intent upon his chosen path. Jacob hoped and prayed that it would bring David the peace which seemed to have evaded him up until now. Ever since David's arrival in Virginia, it had been clear that he was a troubled soul. Jacob missed David, who despite everything he still thought of as his son, but he also felt blessed to have the rest of his extended family around him.

Aside from Jacob's work on the plantation, he always found time to assist his fellow man in whatever way he could, always with an open heart and mind, as he and Elizabeth had done growing up together and in the years that they were married. His children and grandchildren grew up learning from him and were inspired by his desire to help those less fortunate. The twins in particular were especially altruistic by nature.

Benjamin had fully embraced the religion of his father and over the years had studied Torah and its teachings, so much so that he became a rabbi and founded Virginia's first ever synagogue. He worked a great deal to help educate plantation owners of their responsibility to treat their slaves with humanity.

Jacob and David communicated by mail over the years until one day a letter arrived and Jacob decided that the time had come for him to pay a visit to his son. Jacob and Abby realised that if they did not make the trip soon then it would be too late, so they planned a journey which would take them first to Jerusalem, next to Bombay and on to Tibet.

In Jerusalem they met up with Ahmed and his son Mustafa. The life-threatening situation they had shared back in Guinea had formed an unbreakable bond and they rejoiced at being reunited. Mustafa and Ahmed were only too delighted to meet Abby and to introduce the couple to their own wives, children and extended family, coming together for a feast in honour of their overseas guests. It was particularly poignant for Jacob to meet his namesake, Mustafa's firstborn son and to find that he was hailed as somewhat of a hero for his actions so long ago when they were attacked by the roadside.

During their visit to Jerusalem, Mustafa and Ahmed accompanied Jacob and Abby, in traditional dress, to the Temple Mount and the Western Wall. In all his days and throughout his travels, Jacob had never before experienced a feeling as profound as that which he felt standing in this most sacred of places, absorbing the power of the holy site. Neither Abby or Jacob had ever felt so spiritually in touch with the religion they shared, and the encounter would remain with them for the rest of their lives.

From Jerusalem, their next stop was Bombay visiting Raja and his family. Jacob's heart filled with pride as Doctor Raja, as he was now known, introduced him to his wife and their two children, and told him about the work he was doing to assist orphans and street children in the city. It was clear to Jacob that Doctor Raja, a humble and yet much-admired man, had the love and respect of his family and the local people.

Onwards to Tibet, Jacob and Abby embarked on the last stage of their travels and after a long sea voyage they journeyed inland with a guide to the isolated mountain village which was home to David. The village could only be reached via steps carved into the side of a snow-capped mountain from which the views of the surrounding countryside were breath-taking, but here the air which filled their lungs felt purer than any they had breathed before.

Their arrival in the village was greeted by bemused looks from its residents who were clearly not familiar with foreigners, but when their guide enquired on their behalf about David, everyone seemed to know who he was. It seemed that David was known in the village as Pala, meaning father, and was particularly revered for his work with children and the needy.

At the temple Jacob and Abby's guide spoke to one of the monks, asking him to inform David that his father and step-mother were here to see him. It was some hours later that David emerged from the temple, barely recognisable with his shaven head and maroon coloured robe. Choked with the emotion of the reunion, all three embraced each other wordlessly and immediately Jacob and Abby could sense the change within David. Here was a man at peace with himself and with his god, his energy was very much in the light and no longer residing in the shadows.

Jacob reached into the pocket of his waistcoat and pulled out his old gold pocket watch and a necklace. Taking David's hand in his, Jacob gently placed the watch in David's open palm, smiling warmly at him as he did so. David carefully opened the watch to see a miniature portrait of his beautiful mother then brought the watch to his chest, bowing his head in memory of her. When he looked up again Jacob placed the necklace over David's head and around his neck. The pendent was a Star of David.

Standing face to face, placing his hands upon his shoulders, Jacob looked into David's eyes and in them he saw Elizabeth.

"One day my son, when you are ready to come home, we will be waiting to welcome you back to the family. There will always be a home for you in Virginia. We will never give up hope of you coming back to us."

Jacob embraced David and held him in his arms for the longest time, hoping beyond hope that this farewell would not be goodbye, but content that he had made his peace with the man he would always regard as his son, no matter what.

Acknowledgements

I would like to thank the following people for their support:

David P Perlmutter
Julie Tucker
Brian Tehrani
Magdalena Susfal
Megan Wiseman
Miriam Pfeil